An Imprint of Pop!
popbooksonline.com

Explore Music

BAND

by Tyler Gieseke

WELCOME TO DiscoverRoo!

This book is filled with videos, puzzles, games, and more! Scan the QR codes* while you read, or visit the website below to make this book pop.

popbooksonline.com/band

abdobooks.com

Published by Pop!, a division of ABDO, PO Box 398166, Minneapolis, Minnesota 55439. Copyright © 2023 by Abdo Consulting Group, Inc. International copyrights reserved in all countries. No part of this book may be reproduced in any form without written permission from the publisher. DiscoverRoo™ is a trademark and logo of Pop!.

Printed in the United States of America, North Mankato, Minnesota.
102022
012023

Cover Photo: Getty Images
Interior Photos: Shutterstock Images; Getty Images; ZUMA Press, Inc. / Alamy Stock Photo
Editor: Grace Hansen
Series Designer: Colleen McLaren

Library of Congress Control Number: 2022941246

Publisher's Cataloging-in-Publication Data
Names: Gieseke, Tyler, author.
Title: Band / by Tyler Gieseke
Description: Minneapolis, Minnesota : Pop!, 2023 | Series: Explore music | Includes online resources and index.
Identifiers: ISBN 9781098243319 (lib. bdg.) | ISBN 9781098244019 (ebook)
Subjects: LCSH: Music--Juvenile literature. | Bands (Music)--Juvenile literature. | Orchestras and bands--Juvenile literature. | History and music--Juvenile literature.
Classification: DDC 785.1--dc23

*Scanning QR codes requires a web-enabled smart device with a QR code reader app and a camera.

TABLE OF CONTENTS

CHAPTER 1
Explore Music. 4

CHAPTER 2
What Is Band?. 10

CHAPTER 3
Conductor and Sections 16

CHAPTER 4
Marching and Grooving 24

Making Connections. 30
Glossary 31
Index. 32
Online Resources 32

CHAPTER 1

EXPLORE MUSIC

A marching band moves across the field during **halftime** at a football game. The band members wear brightly colored uniforms. They form shapes or words by standing in different patterns. It is exciting and fun.

WATCH A VIDEO HERE!

Many colleges have marching bands with fancy uniforms.

A much smaller band plays in a restaurant. The band's music uses unusual **rhythms** and light, wandering **melodies**. The music is meant to create an easygoing mood for listeners.

Hitting drums can lower stress.

Music is an important part of human **culture**. People have sung notes, drummed out beats, and made instruments for thousands of years. Music can express emotion. It can make an event feel special. Or, it can just be fun for people. There is a lot to explore in the world of music.

Bone flutes existed in China more than 7,000 years ago!

Music comes in many different types.

People can sing and play instruments.

They can even use a computer to make

music. A band is one kind of group

Bands are popular at schools.

that makes music. A band usually has a conductor and groups of different instruments. Some bands play only **jazz** music, and some march while they play.

WHAT IS BAND?

The word *band* is a broad term for a group of **musicians** who make music together. But when people talk about band, they usually mean a concert band. A concert band has a conductor,

The word *band* comes from the French word *bande*, which means "troop" in English.

School concert bands perform a few times each year.

woodwind instruments, brass instruments, and percussion instruments. Concert bands do not have string instruments.

Adults of all ages play in community bands.

Bands have been around for hundreds of years. Some of the first bands appeared in Germany in the

1500s and 1600s. These bands often had woodwind instruments like oboes and bassoons. Armies used to use brass instruments to scare their enemies. Brass bands also helped soldiers march at the same **pace**.

Today, many bands are concert bands. They practice playing songs and then perform them at concerts. Some adults play in a band as part of their jobs. But many bands are made of students or community members. These band members play for free.

JOHN PHILIP SOUSA

John Philip Sousa was born in Washington, DC, in 1854. His father was a Marine Band member. John learned from the band as a teenager. In 1880, he became its 17th leader. He wrote 136 marches before he died in 1932.

One famous band is "The President's Own" United States Marine Band. The band started in 1798 and is the oldest musical group in the US. It plays music for the US president and for official events. John Philip Sousa led the band in the 1880s. He wrote several famous marching songs for band, including "Semper Fidelis."

The US Marine Band marches in New York City.

CHAPTER 3
CONDUCTOR AND SECTIONS

A concert band is made up of a conductor and usually three sections of instruments. The conductor stands in front of the band. He or she does not play an instrument. Instead, the conductor waves a **baton** in a pattern. All the band members play at the speed the baton is waving.

EXPLORE LINKS HERE!

KEEPING TIME

Many pieces of music are played with four beats.

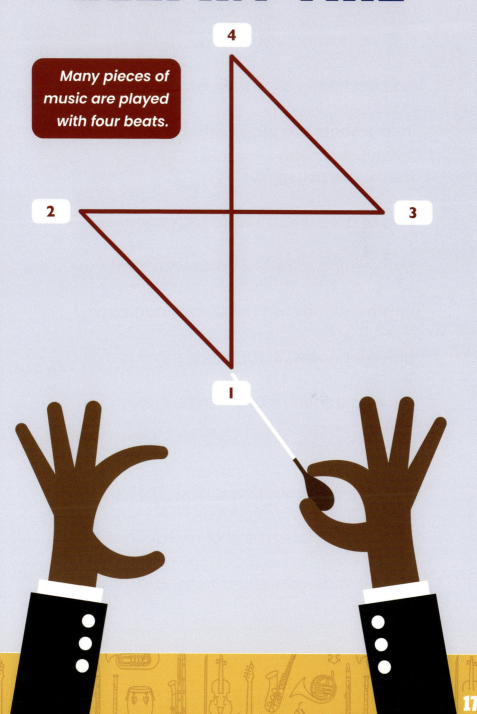

Woodwind instruments make up one section in a concert band. These instruments are pipes with holes in them. The **musician** blows air into one end of the instrument to make sound. By covering different holes with their fingers, woodwind musicians can play different notes. Woodwinds include flutes, clarinets, saxophones, oboes, and bassoons.

The brass section is next. These instruments are made of metal. They have a wide opening on one end. Brass musicians buzz their lips into the other end of the instrument. This makes the sound. Brass musicians make different notes by tightening or loosening their lips. They also press down on the instruments' valve keys. Brass instruments include trumpets, French horns, trombones, baritones, and tubas.

A French horn has three valve keys.

Percussion is the third section of a concert band. People hit or shake percussion instruments to make sound. Some percussion instruments can make a **rhythm** but not different notes. These

Each timpani drum (right) *plays a different note.*

include the snare drum and cymbals. The timpani and the xylophone are percussion instruments that can play different notes. Musicians hit panels on a xylophone to play **melodies**.

EXPLORE BAND

There is a lot to explore in a concert band. The instruments shown here are common. If you had to pick your top three, what would they be? Why?

CHAPTER 4
MARCHING AND GROOVING

There are other types of band besides concert band. A marching band usually has the same instruments as a concert band. But, the **musicians** march around as they play. This is hard work!

DID YOU KNOW? The oldest US college marching band is the University of Notre Dame Band of the Fighting Irish.

This girl plays saxophone in a marching band.

Marching bands are common in parades and football games. Many marching bands come from high schools and colleges.

 **COMPLETE AN ACTIVITY HERE!**

The Ohio State University marching band spells the state's name.

A drum major is the leader of a marching band. The drum major makes sure the band is playing together and marching correctly. When marching bands perform on sports fields, they sometimes stand in patterns that look like letters or images. They might spell out a team's name. Or, they might make the image of a team's **mascot**.

DID YOU KNOW? Jazz is known for improvisation. This is when a jazz musician makes up a **melody** to play on the spot.

Jazz bands are another type of band. These bands typically include piano, trumpet, trombone, saxophone, clarinet, and percussion. Jazz bands play music with special **rhythms**. These rhythms focus on the spaces in between the main beats of a song. This produces a special sound. People like to relax or groove with jazz music.

Bands are popular ways to create and enjoy music. When different musicians and instruments play together, they produce sounds that they couldn't on their own. Concert bands, marching bands, and jazz bands are just a few ways that people explore music.

Jazz music is known for being complex and emotional.

MAKING CONNECTIONS

TEXT-TO-SELF

Would you want to be part of a band? Why or why not?

TEXT-TO-TEXT

What other books have you read about musical groups? How do those compare with this book?

TEXT-TO-WORLD

Have you heard a band perform before? If so, what kind of music did it play? If not, what type of band would you like to go see?

GLOSSARY

baton — a thin rod for leading a musical group.

culture — the arts, beliefs, and ways of life of a group of people.

halftime — a break during the middle of a sports event.

jazz — music with a generally light, smooth quality and offbeat rhythms.

mascot — an animal, person, or sometimes a thing, that stands for a team or group.

melody — the main tune of a song.

musician — someone who plays music.

pace — how quickly or slowly something goes.

rhythm — the length of time and patterns in which sounds are played in a piece of music.

INDEX

brass, 11, 13, 18–19, 23

concert band, 10–11, 13, 16, 18, 20, 22–24, 29

conductor, 9–10, 16

jazz band, 9, 28–29

marching band, 4, 9, 14, 24–25, 27, 29

percussion, 11, 20–22, 28

Sousa, John Philip, 14

sports, 4, 25, 27

United States Marine Band, 14

woodwind, 11, 13, 18, 23

DiscoverRoo!
ONLINE RESOURCES

This book is filled with videos, puzzles, games, and more! Scan the QR codes* while you read, or visit the website below to make this book pop.

popbooksonline.com/band

*Scanning QR codes requires a web-enabled smart device with a QR code reader app and a camera.